falling sky

written and illustrated by
benjamin dickson

FALLING SKY

Written and Illustrated by Benjamin Dickson.

- -

Printed in the UK by Warpton Creative, in partnership with Smallzone.

Published by Scar Comics.

Distributed by Smallzone.

For information on other Scar Comics publications, please visit www.scarcomics.com.

ISBN: 0-9553697-0-3
978-0-9553697-0-4

- -

For more information on Falling Sky, including how and why it was written and illustrated, information on Near-Earth Objects and more, please visit the Falling Sky website at:

www.bendickson.co.uk/fallingsky

LONDON, 3:20PM. 44 HOURS TO IMPACT.

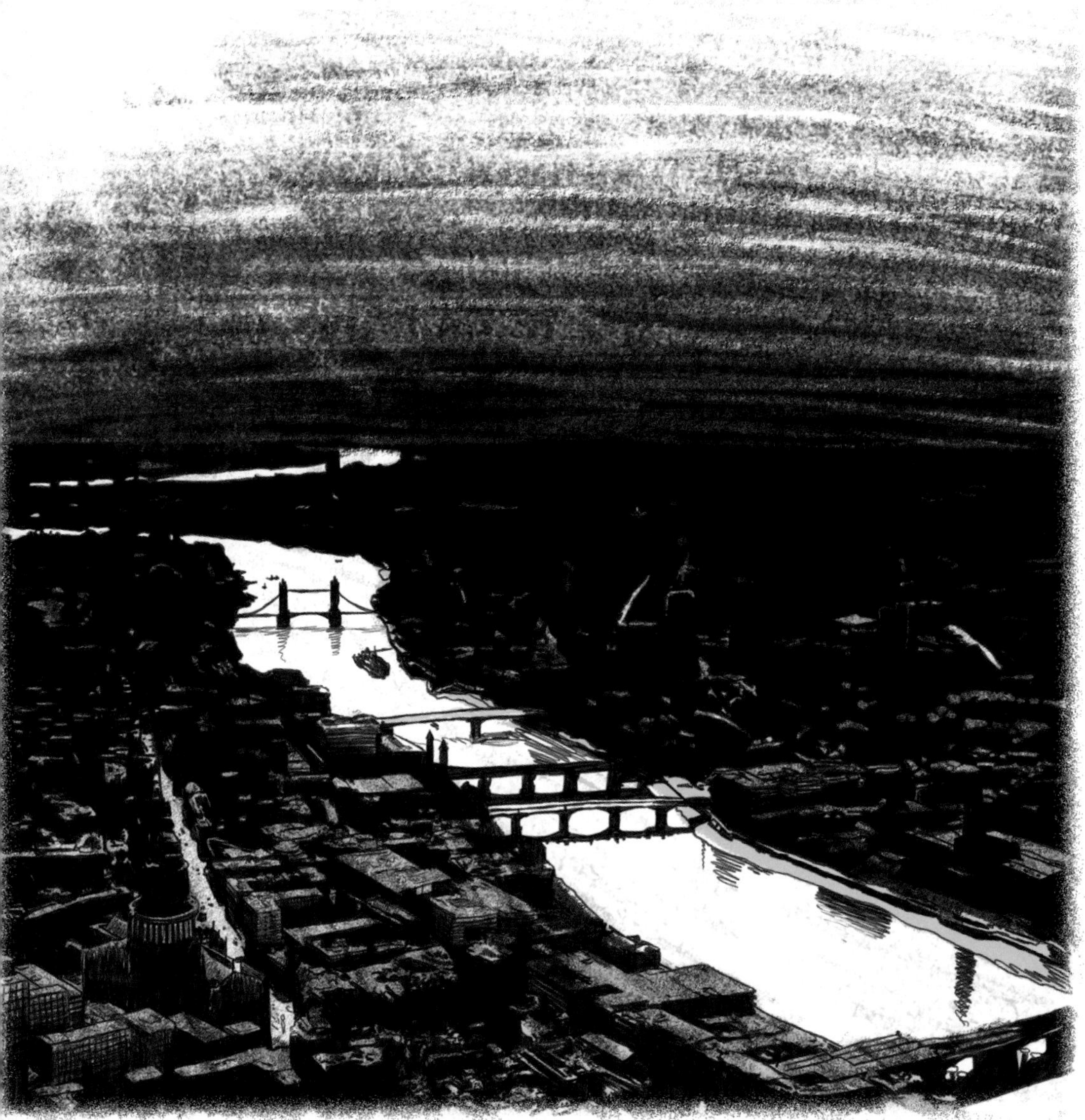

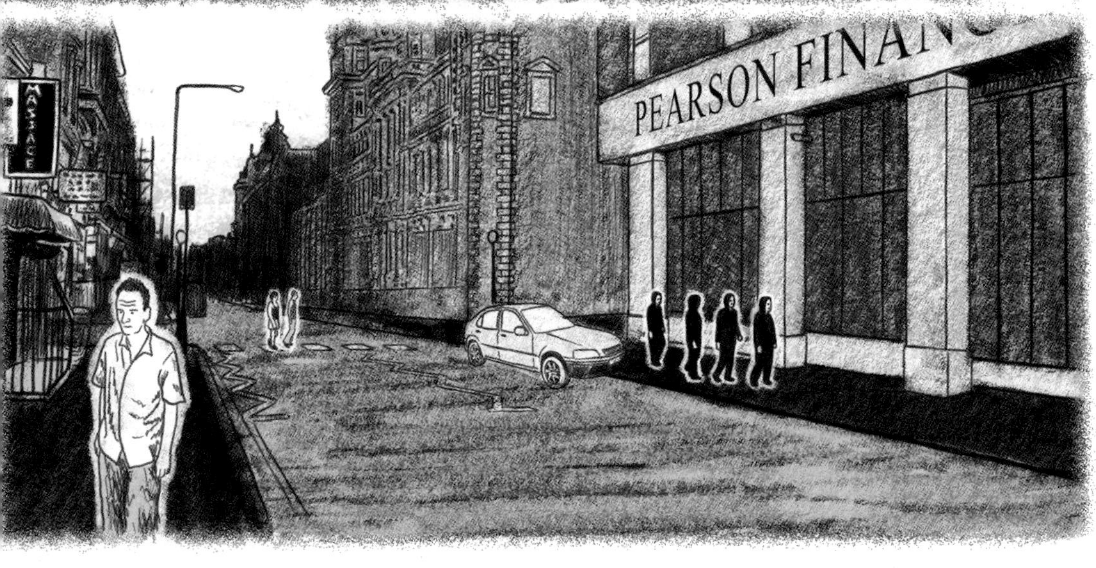

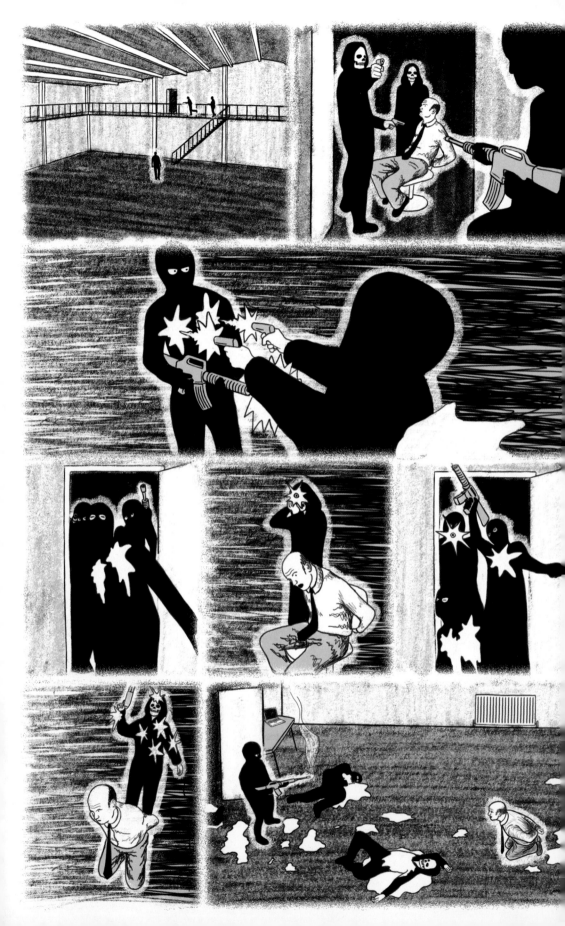

6:03AM. 28 HOURS TO IMPACT.

PEOPLE ARE STARING AT US.

I KNOW. WE NEED TO GET OFF THE STREETS.

DO YOU THINK THEY KNOW ABOUT US?

IT'S POSSIBLE. IF ANYONE HERE IS PART OF THE *RAGNAROK GROUP*, THEN THEY'L KNOW. PLUS THE BLOODHOUNDS ARE LOOKING FOR US.

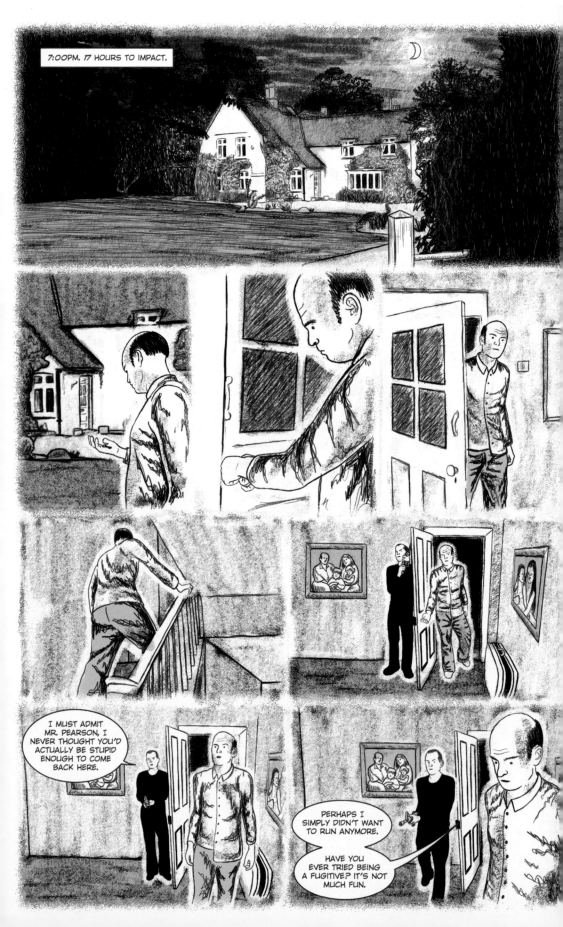

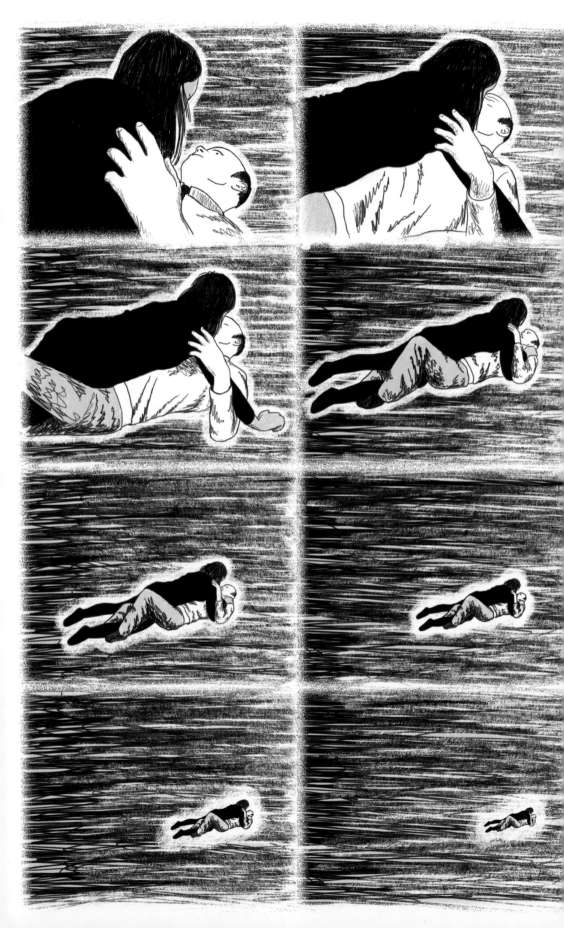

about the author

Benjamin Dickson floated around the outside of the UK independent comics scene for a number of years, refusing to illustrate his own scripts on the basis that he couldn't draw comics. When he did finally take the plunge and set about illustrating an 80-page graphic novel, the feedback he recieved seemed to suggest that he had managed to fool everyone into thinking that he actually could draw comics after all. Nobody was more surprised by this than Ben himself.

A former teacher, web designer, painter, photographer and general artist, Benjamin Dickson lives in Bristol and spends most of his time daydreaming and eating falafels. He has a fondness for Bill Hicks, Pavement albums, Chicken Tikka Masala and nuclear war movies, and has an intense hatred of neck ties, house fires and the song "Love Is All Around" by Wet Wet Wet.

He wrote and illustrated this book in 2003-2005 at the age of 27-29, and hopes to be able to write a few more before the real apocalypse.

Photograph by James Reed.

acknowledgements

This book owes a huge debt of thanks to many people. Firstly, every character in this book has been modelled for by friends and family, without whom this book wouldn't have been possible. The primary characters were:

Laurie Ray as Charles, *Delphine Guillemoteau* as Rijuta, *Caleb Harris* as Edward, my father *Ian Dickson* as the Prime Minister, and *Martin Summers* as General Dye.

The supporting and background characters were played by: *Ben Johns, Richard McGee, Lara Coleman, Jon Stanley, Hamish Kemp, Paul Gravett, Ernie Gartrell, Marc Richards, Wil Player, Craig Peta-Stuart, Robin Weir, Katie Harris, Guss Hargreves, Liz Simmonds, Liz Humphrey, Geoff Norburn, Adam Yoell and Caroline Najsblum.* Heartfelt thanks to all of the above - not just for the loan of their bodies, but also for actually being interested in what I was borrowing them for.

Thanks are especially owed to James McKay, a longtime comics partner and friend, for helping me to initially plot the story in Fenchurch St Station in London in 2003. James was originally going to be the illustrator for the story, and I also thank him for eventually refusing to do so, forcing me to get off my arse and illustrate the damn thing myself.

Thanks are also owed to Paul Gravett for his continual support and encouragement, and to my parents for not telling me that I was too old to read comics. Thanks also to Boo Cook, Chris Staros, Gary Spencer Millidge, William Volley and David Hitchcock for their encouraging feedback, to Barry Renshaw for his support and help with publicity, and of course to Shane Chebsey for publishing the book.

read on...

You can read about the production of this book on the official Falling Sky website, where you'll find information about how the book came about, technical information about the fictional asteroid from Falling Sky, reviews and feedback from readers, and even a musical score to listen to whilst you read the book! Visit:

w w w . b e n d i c k s o n . c o . u k / f a l l i n g s k y